Lost In The Wilderness

A Stella Madison Caper

Lilly Maytree

Lightsmith Publishers
Thorne Bay, Alaska

ISBN: 978-1-944798-50-5

Published in the United States by

Lightsmith Publishers
P.O. Box 19293
Thorne Bay, Alaska 99919

Website: www.LightsmithPublishers.com

Cover photography by Steve and Becky Brown

Lightsmith Publishers is an imprint of the Wilderness School Institute, a non-profit educational organization that offers outdoor youth activities in wilderness settings, including training in wilderness skills and nature studies, as well as the publication of curriculum on related subjects, through the Wilderness School Press, and their children's imprint Summers Island Press.

Lost In The Wilderness / LTB Paperback Edition

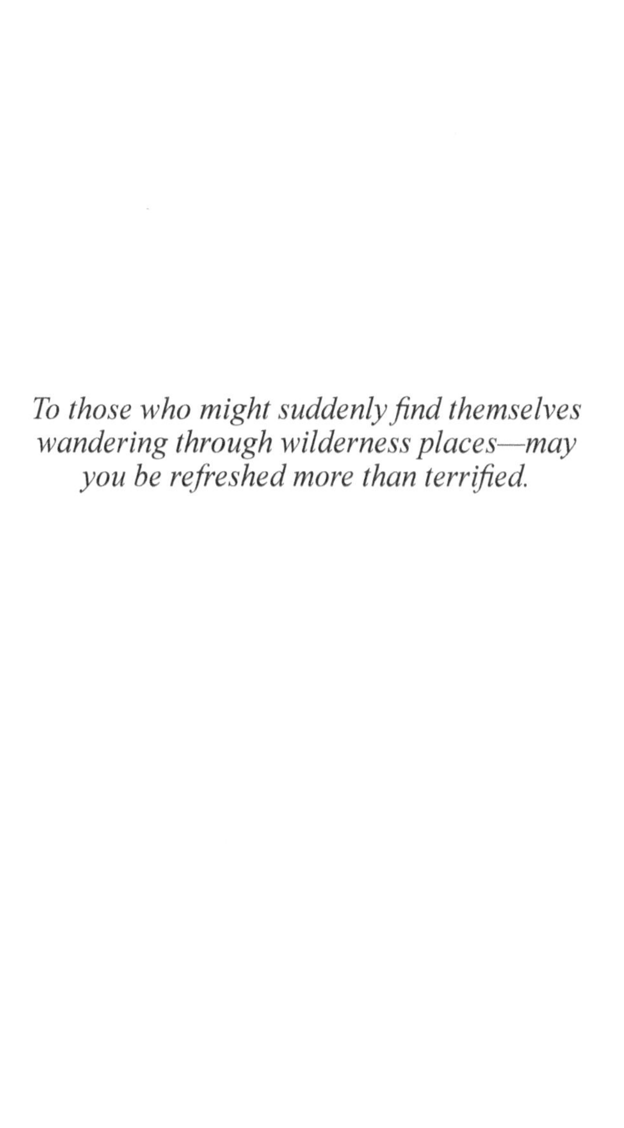

To those who might suddenly find themselves wandering through wilderness places—may you be refreshed more than terrified.

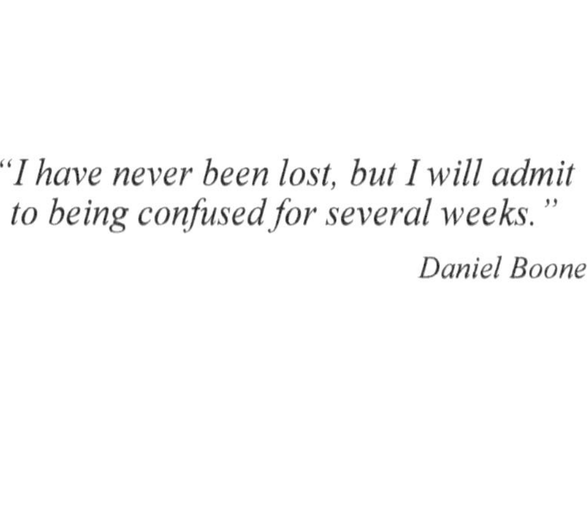

*"I have never been lost, but I will admit
to being confused for several weeks."*

Daniel Boone

1

Stella Madison opened the door to the after-deck and a blast of cold wind hit her face. Why did Millie want to meet out here? The galley of the *Dreadnaught* was so much more comfortable and cozy. Of course there was always someone else passing through it.

"I brought us some tea, Millie." She set the tray down on a small table between two deck lounges.

"Oh, thanks, Stel." Her former landlady set her knitting aside and tightened the black-and-white checkered scarf under her chin that she had wrapped around her auburn hair." Something hot would be good about now."

"It's awfully cold out here." Stella pulled

her periwinkle blue knit cap down lower over her fluffy white hair that was just long enough to tuck under and zipped her jacket all the way up.

"We're in Alaska, now. Mason says we have been ever since we crossed that Dixon Entrance, with all those fishing boats we had to dodge in and out of. Said if we didn't have to go all the way to Ketchikan to get back through customs again, we could be almost to the lodge by now. Mmm... Orange Spice. My favorite."

"Mine's the Moroccan Mint. Except Orange Spice just seemed warmer this morning." She sat down in the other lounge and unfolded a green wool blanket over her lap. "Captain Stuart sure brought home a lot of souvenirs from his Navy days. Every lounge chair on this boat has one of these. Thank goodness."

"They're Army-issue. I think half the things aboard he got from one of those old Army surplus places back home."

"Well, looks aren't everything. They're nice and warm, anyway. Imagine being almost to the lodge, Millie. I can hardly wait to see it."

"Me, too. It will definitely be a load off my mind to get on solid ground, again."

"I thought you liked living on the boat."

"I do. It's got all kinds of ambiance. And that galley is heaven to cook in. It's the ocean I'm scared stiff of. Don't think I ever will get used to it." She set her cup down and picked up her knitting, again.

Stella was about to take another sip of her tea when she realized her friend's project was a sock with such an enormous tube it would go way past a person's knee, already. "Millie, who on earth is that for?"

"This? Oh, it isn't for anybody. I just knit to settle my nerves. The only thing I ever learned to do was socks. Way back when I was ten. Took me half the trip even to remember how to do it because it's been that long since I practiced." As if to prove the point, she began to unravel it, again.

Stella gasped at seeing the thing disappear into a heap of wrinkly gray yarn right before her eyes. "But all that work—wouldn't you rather have something to show for it? Give them away for Christmas, maybe."

"They're not good enough for that. They always turn out crooked or something. But a person has to resort to some form of therapy when they're scared half out of their mind most of the time. Wouldn't you say?"

"I guess it depends on what you're scared of. The colonel says if it's something evil, you just tell it to buzz off, because you don't want anything to do with the dark side of supernatural. But if it's something legitimate like the ocean, I don't blame you. I was scared stiff myself during that storm we had. And I don't like it when it gets rough and choppy, either. But it must at least make you feel better that we're almost there."

"The truth is, Stel, I'm even more scared

about getting there. Because of the bears. Mason says just make a lot of noise and stay in groups. On account of they don't want anything to do with us, either."

"Well, that sounds reasonable, don't you think?"

"Not as reasonable as having a loaded gun on my belt."

Stella wasn't sure if she would be more afraid of Millie walking around with a loaded gun than a bear but she didn't mention it.

"Bears you can shoot. But the ocean..." She got to the end of unraveling her sock and started casting on new stitches, again. "The ocean is so unpredictable and... big. I really don't know how Stuart even finds his way around in it. Especially without radar."

"We don't have radar?"

"Too expensive, and he never had the funds."

"For heaven sake, I didn't know that." She felt a twinge of apprehension at the very thought. "He's so confident about everything,

I just assumed."

"Used to be confident. Which is really why I asked you to come out here, Stel." Millie stopped working, and looked her right in the eye. "Something is wrong with Stuart. He hasn't been himself the last couple of weeks."

"Well, he does have a lot more to worry about than the rest of us. The Dreadful being his boat, and all."

"It's the *Dreadnaught*, not the Dreadful. Sometimes I think you enjoy calling it that."

"I do. It's such a monstrosity of a thing. Although I have to admit it has its charm. I'll probably be won over by the time we finally get there." She took another sip of her tea and noticed Millie had dropped two stitches by the time she went back to her knitting. "But Captain Stuart has such peculiar ways, I don't see how you can tell if he's his normal self or not. He's one of the most abnormal people I've ever known."

"I can tell, all right. He only ate half his

linguine and clams the other night and that's one of his favorite meals. He never used to miss when I made it back home."

"Maybe he's just not used to all our home-cooked meals. Didn't Mason say he lived mostly off boiled eggs, crackers, and sardines?"

"That and junk food. Which is why I decided to make hamburgers and fries for our celebration, tonight. That's his other favorite. The rest of of us won't mind as long as we barbecue and fill things out with your New England baked beans and Lou's fruit salad. If he doesn't eat any of that, we'll know something's definitely wrong. You think?"

"I'm thinking what would we do if anything happened to Captain Stuart. Maybe the rest of us should try to carry more of the load for a while. Could be he's coming down with something and just needs a rest."

"Could be. But I'm going to keep my eye on him during our Alaska celebration. Then slip him a good physic if I think he isn't quite right."

"Why, Millie—that's an awful thing to do to somebody. You should ask, first."

"He wouldn't take it at all, if I asked. Better just to slip it into his tea."

The celebration started somewhat early that night because the fog rolled in so thick they were forced to pull over into the nearest cove and anchor. Such places were numerous throughout the islands, and they were pure wilderness. Something that had little effect—other than offering spectacular scenery from every angle—to the small community of friends aboard the *Dreadnaught*.

Even fuel stations, which were few and far between the farther north they got, didn't really matter so much. Captain Stuart said they had enough to make the entire trip just on their original fill-up back in California. It was the one thing they wouldn't scrimp on and the main reason they opted to all sign on for extra "shipboard duties," rather than go to the added expense of hiring a professional crew. They also had the option of using the sails, which cut down considerably on fuel expenses all by itself.

Except there hadn't been much opportunity to use those sails. Going north, the wind was almost always "right on their nose," as the Captain called it, instead of on either side or behind them, where they could actually get some use out of it. Not to mention a sailboat of this size took practically a full gale to get it really moving (having been built more for ocean crossings). Not that they hadn't had to wait out a lot of gale-force weather pocketed away in some deserted place like this one. It's just that the combination of narrow channels, crazy strong currents and tides—as well as those gale-force winds—made for nightmare situations with such a novice crew. No matter how good everyone's intentions were.

Yes, Captain Stuart most probably had a lot on his mind.

Stella was thinking about all these things as she took her pot of New England baked beans out of the oven and set it at the back of the stove to keep warm. The men were out under a covered portion of the deck, overseeing the barbecue, and Millie was busy setting the huge table. Which looked especially lovely with the overhead kerosene lamp lit (dark clouds had moved in and it was already starting to rain) and a little blue pot of artificial white daisies the two of them had picked up in some dollar store at their last stop in Canada. Now, with nearly all of the long trip behind them, and their crossing back over into the U.S. earlier this afternoon, it was time to celebrate. They were finally in Alaska!

Even Millie seemed to have forgotten her dark worries of the morning, and cheerfully tucked one of those white daisies, that had fallen out of its setting, into her bountiful

French twist as she hummed the same two lines of the old fifties classic, *Blueberry Hill*, over and over, again.

About then, Lou Edna, Cole, and the Senator came in from the forward companionway.

"Oh, my word!" Stella exclaimed as the little toddler with the big name reached out his arms to her. "If you aren't dressed like a regular little boy—rubber boots and everything!" She took him from Cole, who seemed especially cleaned up, himself, not missing the fact the two were both wearing jeans and the same blue sweatshirts.

"Cole says he won't know he's a boy unless we dress him like one." Lou Edna reached for another denim apron that hung just inside the walk-in pantry. "Besides that, he wore holes in the knees of all his bunny suits already, from crawling around so much."

"Wouldn't surprise me if he was walking before the month's out." Millie took the little boy from Stella when he reached out to her as soon as she got close enough. "Right, luvy? How about some fruit salad? It'll be awhile before those hamburgers are done, Lou."

"I'll just give him a cold hotdog."

"A baby can't grow strong living off potato chips and hotdogs. Wouldn't you say so, Stella?"

"Well, I wouldn't know so much about that," she replied. "But, as a teacher, I have heard it said that not having enough proteins and enzymes in the diet can lean toward tendencies of ADD. Which leads to behavior problems. Then—nine times out of ten—the authorities have to step in."

There was an audible gasp from Lou, as Stella had expected, since the young woman knew exactly what having to live under the supervision of authorities meant.

Cole, who hadn't said a word during the entire exchange, reached for an apple from the fruit bowl on the counter, and gave her an appreciative wink before heading out the opposite door to join the men. By that time, Lou had her apron tied and was rummaging through the refrigerator for the fruit salad. Her blonde hair was gathered at the nape of her neck with a beige "scrunchie" that was a perfect match to the angora pull-over sweater which seemed somewhat the opposite of her usual t-shirt, jeans, and sweatshirt. She even had a set of lovely, teardrop pearl earrings on.

Then again, it was an evening of celebration and Stella thought it rather touching that she had even gone so far as to change the baby out of his usual pajama attire. Lou Edna had come a long way since her heartfelt decision to get on the right side of life (and the law) and change her ways. After a couple of weeks, the effects of the relief alone was softening her into a real beauty. The kind that came from inner peace instead of outward application. Come to think of it, considering how she used to get so overly made-up for her bank job every day, Stella couldn't remember seeing any of that once they all moved aboard the *Dreadnaught*.

Having made a mental note to keep an eye on whether or not Captain Stuart ate his dinner, was forgotten about halfway through the meal. It was during the discussion of what everyone's plans for the evening were. Usually, they lingered over coffee and dessert, swapping entertaining stories from varied backgrounds. However, if it was a weekend, or an occasion for celebration such as this one, they might go so far as to play a game of "Rummy," using shipboard tokens in lieu of cash, that could be traded for chores, favors, or some coveted food item a person might have a hankering for. Another favorite was to listen to some true account read from one of the volumes of hero stories that the colonel had chronicled over his years as a military historian.

Every bit of which went to the wayside when Lou Edna announced they had something entirely different in mind for this particular evening. If the Captain would agree.

"I got no complaints about most shipboard entertainments," he replied, adding more ketchup to a pile of French fries that was larger than his hamburger. "Long as it's legal."

"Lou and I were wondering if you'd marry us." Cole looked directly into the startled glance of the disheveled older man across the table. "You've done that before, haven't you?"

"I have. Got the service printed out in the back of my old Seafarer's Bible. Along with funerals and other such things a captain might need to preside over."

"Well, then?"

"I think it's a fine idea," said the colonel. "Nothing seals a promise so much as an act that truly proves your commitment. It's the kind of trust between parties that one can't get any other way. More importantly, it's the right thing to do."

"I want to do everything right from now

on." Lou Edna picked up a French fry the baby had deliberately thrown onto the floor and put it back on the tray of his high chair. "If doing things right could make you feel this good—how come nobody ever told me?"

"For one thing, you never let anyone tell you anything," said Mason. "As I recall."

"Neither do you, Pop," the girl countered. "Or you'd have married Millie a long time, ago."

"Lou Edna Wilson!" Millie gasped. "Mase isn't the marrying kind. He's always been up front about that."

"Something's either right, or it isn't," she muttered, bending down for yet another French fry that was gleefully pitched off the tray.

"Living by our convictions should always supersede trying to convince others to live by them, as well," the colonel pointed out. "Seems everyone's entitled to their own journey of discovery, no matter where it happens to land them. But as you found out so recently, Lou, some roads are more rocky than others."

"Wasn't my choice to be born there."

"No one else gets that choice, either. The only choice available is in getting off, or not. But it might help to know all roads lead to the same end. So, the fact that yours looked so much clearer, earlier on, will probably give you an advantage some of the rest of us—who chose later in life—never had."

A statement that launched an unguarded expression of satisfaction at Mason when Lou Edna looked back at him. And since everyone had rather naturally taken to considering the colonel the best source of spiritual judgment in their little group (simply because he had been working at it longer), the verdict, though unspoken, was pronounced. Something that caused the colonel to draw in his breath and stick out his lower lip in that expression of perplexity that was becoming so dear to Stella (such a tender-hearted man!). Because the last thing he would ever want to do was offend Mason, who was one of his original heroes.

So, there were a few awkward moments of silence when even the colonel was at a loss for words. Until Mason suddenly banged his fist down on the table and pronounced, "Shortcake's right. Better make it a double, Stuart. So I can make an honest woman out of Mildred. Haven't been very happy with my own road, lately... and I could do with some of this peace and contentment I been seeing around here."

A sentiment that caused Millie to burst immediately into tears, and the baby right after.

At the precise moment Gerald pushed through the door from the outside deck with another plate of sizzling burgers and asked, "Anybody for seconds? Oh—I say! Now, what's wrong?"

And that was the reason—as Stella was to recall later—that nearly everyone's plate was left with something on it that evening.

Especially since they decided to push things aside for later, and fully intended to come back to it all. Except that when Stuart returned from his cabin (presumably to get the old Seafarer's Bible, to officiate services), a rather amazing transformation had taken place.

For the first time in the nearly two months they had been aboard the *Dreadnaught*, Captain Stuart appeared before them in a rather dashing black coat over a turtleneck sweater, with his gray hair that normally stuck out in all directions, slicked back and curling fashionably onto his collar. And considering Millie had scampered away to don a cheery floral-print dress (instead of jeans), and even Mason quickly shaved off his three-day bristle of whiskers and put on a clean denim shirt...

The unexpected occasion turned into a series of memorable tender moments that "the family" would never forget. It was their first day in Alaska, and in so many ways, their first day of a new way of life for all of them. So, the services—instigated by the youngest members (who would have thought?) --took place on the covered deck beneath the wheelhouse with all the rugged beauty of a mountain wilderness for a backdrop. There were even a few appreciative hugs and comments, afterward, for Lou Edna's determination to "do things right" that had propelled everyone to share in the whole wonderful experience.

Which could have been a perfect end to a perfect day.

Except just as they were all dispersing toward the various companionway doors that led out of the galley and toward their respective cabins, Lou Edna said, "Just in time, too. Because I'm going to have another baby."

Stella and the colonel stopped in their tracks, and Millie's, "Oh—Lou—Edna!" reverberated back toward them down the entire length of the hallway. That shocking news delivered so casually to those born with different values altogether, was the very reason the nightly ritual of listening to the weather channel was skipped, entirely. After all, they weren't on any specific schedule (other than their own), and tomorrow was another day.

There would be plenty enough time to get those necessary details in the morning.

The following morning they were socked in by a veritable "pea souper," as the Captain called it. One couldn't even see the trees on the edge of the nearby shore of the cove they were anchored in. Other than the first twinge of disappointment (they were so close to reaching their goal!), everyone soon settled into their various routines with the sort of resigned contentment that comes from having to wait on things one has no control over. There was always something to do and the same situation had happened to them on numerous occasions before.

So, the Captain and Cole took the

opportunity to do some necessary maintenance on the engine, and Mason went back to carpenter-work on an overhead lighting project that connected two nightstands together, so Millie could get more reading done at night. She was working her way through Stella's library, even though she had never been much of a reader before.

Lou Edna, who rarely made an appearance before noon, had not so much as poked her head out of the spacious apartment she had made from the former crew's quarters in the lowest forward area of the ship. She had created a huge, rather ingenious play area for the baby that allowed for climbing over and between the various bunks via a cargo net tacked up and over them to prevent falls. With a collection of toys scattered within, and an occasional snack, he was happy to entertain himself until lunchtime.

Gerald was busy with his numerous studies of the many potted plants he had brought along. Who could tell which ones would thrive in such a climate? He had heard common vegetables could grow to enormous sizes in a place that had nearly twenty hours of sunlight per day this time of year. He was meticulously detailed in his charts and scientific journals. Such still being one of his few joys in life since he had retired from the academic world, years ago.

As for Stella and the colonel, this was the best time of their day. The new book was coming along nicely and it seemed its author had never had such fun until he took up writing stories for boys. And with a wife to edit his rough drafts, who enjoyed bouncing new ideas around almost as much as he did, he was never happier. What's more, he was convinced—after all these years—he had truly discovered what he was not only best at, but made for. If one were to believe in that sort of thing. Which Stella did. Taking on his ambitions and philosophies had been as easy as taking his name. Mrs. Colonel Oliver P. Henry. She had never been happier in her life, either.

So the colonel was sitting at the old captain's desk, getting ready to enjoy an extra writing session since he would not have to take his stint at the wheel today. "Let's see..." He bent over the handwritten jottings in an open notebook where he had written his outline. "What are you boys up to next?" He ran a finger down to the appropriate place. "Ah, yes. The cave. You think you might find a good place to stash necessary supplies in case the whole world goes berserk. Well..." He opened his laptop and waited for it to take account of itself. "Think, again! Just wait till you see what's waiting for you in there!" Then he laughed with the pure pleasure of it and began.

Stella smiled from where she was sitting on the couch with her own laptop, going over his work from the day before. For a moment, she paused to think about several things that might be in such a cave... and then went back to the enjoyable task at hand. She had always loved reading stories for the middle-grades, and—after her years of teaching—knew quite a bit about boys, herself.

It was hardly an hour after that when they heard the thump of the engine starting up.

"What's all this?" remarked the colonel as he threw a look to the bank of French windows behind where Stella was sitting. "It's still socked in out there."

At which point there was a tremendous bang from somewhere in the depths of the vessel.

"Oliver—oh, what on earth?"

"Probably just Stuart readjusting his engine again, dearest. But maybe I better go make sure."

A few minutes later it seemed to be humming along just fine and a few minutes after that, it shut off, again. Stella breathed a sigh of relief that they wouldn't have to be venturing out in that pea souper after all, before she realized her own nerves were almost as stretched as Millie's. Captain

Stuart's propensity to "nose out into the weather to see what it was going to do," was beginning to grate on her.

So, she felt even better when her husband reappeared a few minutes later to report, "Just changing out some hard-to-get-at hose, then using some kind of starter fluid that produces a big bang. Sort of a controlled burn, you might say. No need to worry."

"Well, thank heaven for that. It would be awful to have something go wrong when we only have a little farther to go."

"Indeed, it would."

However, the day only proceeded to get stranger from that point on. It was one of those days people find themselves considering whether they shouldn't have gone back to get up on the opposite side of the bed, in order to straighten things out. Because Stuart—always so careful to "do things by the book,"—suddenly decided to strike out across their last stretch of "big water," late in the afternoon. The Ketchikan Channel (not what it was formally called, but no one could pronounce the real name) being only about five hours away. Piece of cake after that because it was such a busy city, one merely had to follow a crowd of other boats back into the harbor. And considering it would still be daylight at nine pm, not much could go wrong.

The first thing that went wrong was a large rock at the entrance of their cove, which had been clearly visible when they came in, but was now covered over with a high tide. Even though the accidental bumping against it didn't cause any real damage, it served as a wake-up call to remind them of the necessity of having a spotter at the bow when entering or exiting such places. Rocks being the prevailing characteristic of the region. Why the depth sounder didn't give an alarm, no one thought to ask, because maneuvering in and out of tight places had always been the Captain's responsibility. In fact, if he hadn't been at the wheel that very moment, the danger might have caused serious damage.

Things simply went downhill from there. The afternoon wind kicked up stronger than expected, and Stuart's decision to skirt a little farther south of the fishing boats to avoid all those thousands of feet of net strung out across every available space on the U.S. side of Dixon Entrance, drove the *Dreadnaught* into six to eight foot waves, farther out. Why on earth had they even tried to attempt it at this hour?

That's what Stella was thinking when the ship's bell summoned "all hands on deck" to hoist sails.

Heading directly north was no longer an option. Now, they must use the wind to stabilize the ship so they could plow through the waves instead of rolling into the steep troughs each time they were hit from the side. They were sailing directly out into rough weather, and another storm at sea. However, the crew was more seasoned this time and understood their jobs much better than those early days. Which was the only reason they managed to "beat into it" for nearly three full hours before finally raising a distant shore where they could find another safe cove or inlet, to slip into. Who cared how far off course they were? Everyone was exhausted.

Something that only added to the strain on nerves when the place began to disappear on and off, behind patches of clinging fog the wind was still trying to blow off the rugged land. So, they took a compass bearing on a point that looked promising and strained all eyes for any sign of unexpected rocks that might be strewn out in front of it. At least the seas began to settle down the closer they got to land. But so did the wind. Down with the sails, again, and the last hour was a nightmare, before Lou Edna (who had the best eyes aboard) called out a possible opening. A tight squeeze, but they would have to take it.

Because night was already coming on.

So, they began to snake their way up a

long, narrow inlet that seemed to have no sign of widening out, at all. Cole stood at the very tip of the bowsprit, giving hand-signals up to the wheelhouse as they inched their way around the rocky shores at a snail's pace.

"Over there!" Lou called down from her perch on the mainmast yardarm. "Big enough to turn around in!"

"Port, or starboard?" insisted Cole.

"On the right—the right—I mean, starboard!"

He gave the signal but there was no response from the wheelhouse. "Get down here and take over, Lou. Colonel and Mase— get ready to let go the anchor. Millie, keep an eye out for rocks off the port side and holler out soon as you see any. Mrs. H, you come with me."

Which is how it came to be that Stella was the only witness to exactly what happened, next.

She followed Cole up the short steep ladder to the topmost deck of the

Dreadnaught (lagging considerably behind the quick agility of their dark-haired First Mate), and was shocked to arrive in time to see him thrust the older man aside and take over the wheel so forcibly that their captain fell into a crumpled heap onto the floor. She had read enough sea stories to know such an act was nothing less than mutiny, but didn't know exactly what she should do about it. Other than rushing to the side of Captain Stuart, only to discover that he was completely unconscious.

At which point there was an ear-splitting scream of "Rocks! Rocks!" from Millie, before Cole immediately spun the wheel hard over and...ran right over them.

Stella was picking herself up off the floor before she even realized she had toppled over. There was screaming and hollering (Millie, mostly) and a tumult of running feet clamoring over the decks below. Were they sinking? By the time she pulled herself up enough to look over at Cole, the young man was standing with his back to her, his head sagging down to his chest, and still hanging onto the wheel. But only for a few moments before he gave a great sigh and shut off the engine.

"Is he alive?" he finally asked without turning to see for himself.

"I..." She was still on her knees, and only

had to lean over to look at Stuart. He seemed to be sleeping. She gave his shoulder a gentle shake but there was no response. "I think so. Yes, he's breathing, anyway. Cole—what on earth possessed you to push him so—"

"Something happened. He was froze to the wheel."

"Dear Lord..." She patted the Captain's face, trying once more to wake him. "Maybe we better not move him right away. At least not for a while." She took off her jacket and slipped it under his head, then reached for the army blanket on the nearest chair, to unfold over him.

"I better go check how much damage there is."

He slipped out the door, and was barely gone when Gerald clamored in from the companionway that led from the galley beneath them. He was wearing a bright orange life-jacket, and carrying the Senator over his shoulder, buckled into a miniature of the same. "Millie's gone over the side," he panted. "Saw the whole thing from the galley port when we were getting into our life-jackets. Just—pffft!—popped over like a cork out of a bottle because she was leaning out over the rail too far."

"For heaven sake! Is she—"

"Pfft! Just like that! Had her lifeline on, though, so they hauled her right up. Didn't even get wet, that's how high up we are. What happened to Stuart?"

"We're not sure. Cole said he was frozen. Just hanging onto the wheel." She moved over to where she could look down on the forward deck. It was tilted back at a slight angle and looked eerily deserted. Where was everybody? Were they sinking? What if they had to abandon ship out in this—oh, dear God!

All at once, a single shaft of light broke through the dark clouds as the sun was going down between two magnificent mountain peaks. It gave the illusion of resting right on top of the *Dreadnaught*. In that light it looked as if their ship had nosed close up into a narrow meadow nestled between those two pine- covered mountains. And—what was that? A waterfall tumbling down from somewhere high up, over a wall of rock, not too far away.

Stella felt a sudden sense of profound peace, along with the fleeting thought they had landed in the prettiest place they had come to, yet. Then it occurred to her how often their situation could change (so instantly!) after she prayed for God to save them out of some circumstance that seemed to be pressing her beyond her own personal limits. Almost before she even knew what to pray for. As if simply calling out to God during those times was enough for Him to intervene.

Gerald handed her the baby, and then bent down to have a better look at the Captain. "Seems like he's...had some kind of stroke."

"Oh, I hope not!" She settled the toddler onto her hip. "It could be hours before we can get any kind of help way out here." "More than that I'm afraid. Something busted up forward. Right under the boy's play area. I daresay there was water trickling in when we left."

Stella felt her stomach lurch as if she had just gone down fast in an elevator. "Are we—sinking?"

"Nobody's sinking," replied Mason, who came in at that very moment to switch on the VHF radio. "Just knocked a board loose because somebody didn't know right from left. What are you trying to do, Gerry—scare the women?"

"Best to plan for the worst, I always say."

"Well don't. Cole's got the pumps going, already, and the Colonel's setting up the tools. We'll have it fixed even before help can get here for Stuart. How's he doing? Cole said he passed out for a while."

"A while—he hasn't come out of it, yet." Stella informed him. "Gerry thinks it might be a stroke."

Mason's face registered a combination of remorse and despair as he looked over at his long-time friend, lying so still beneath the green blanket. But only for a moment. After that, he returned his attentions to the radio with renewed vigor. "What's wrong with this thing?" He banged on it and twisted a few more dials. "Probably been busted for years, like everything else around here!"

Gerald's face went pale beneath his black Navy watch-cap. "If we can't call for an emergency helicopter..." His brown mustache quivered. "How the—devil—do we abandon ship?"

"We can't abandon ship," Mason sluffed out of his army- green rain-jacket, now that he was inside and dropped it on a chair. "We've got everything we own on here."

At which point Stella felt her knees go weak and murmured something about getting a bottle for the baby, so she could at least find some place to pull herself together. Anything to keep from being overwhelmed at the thought of being shipwrecked.

Shipwrecked! Right out in the middle of... why, she hadn't the faintest idea where they were in the middle of. And without Stuart to figure it out...

It was a quiet, sombre crew that sat around the table in the galley, two hours later.

The situation was more grim than they first realized. They had set up a cot in one corner so they could bring the Captain in and keep a close eye on him. He still couldn't be wakened. In the meantime, they discovered that not only did the radio in the wheelhouse not work, neither did the weather radio in the galley. Considering they weren't getting much more than static across all channels, they wondered if they might be too closed- in by surrounding trees and mountains to get any reception. They tried to send out a message anyway, but there was no response.

After two months aboard the *Dreadnaught*, they knew enough to get the ship into some safe harbor, even if they didn't know exactly where they were. Or, at least close enough to some fishing boat to ask for help. Except they were stuck fast on top of the rocks they had run over. A fact that turned out to be their salvation, considering the damage had been more extensive than they first realized. While water was only trickling into Lou's apartment, it was fairly pouring into the lower hold, where most of their supplies were. The jolt had opened up a larger crack between the boards, down there.

It might have spelled disaster if the water hadn't stopped rising when it reached a level of two feet at the lowest end of the vessel. This because they had run high enough up on the rocks to be about three-quarters out of the water everywhere else. Which should have made them feel safer. Except the knowledge that the water fell off to depths of nearly a hundred feet on either side, made them realize where they might have been—this very minute—if they hadn't run so hard aground.

Something they had to credit to Cole for thinking so fast. But while they were not sunk, they were definitely not going anywhere. At least not anytime soon. Maybe even never, if the tide didn't rise sufficiently to float them back off the rocks, again. And even though there was always the hope that someone else might wander into this same place and find them, who knew how long that would take? The only thing they did know was they were in some wild corner of the Pacific Ocean where most of the of the smaller islands they had been traveling through were uninhabited.

And there were hundreds of them.

Of course, there was always the possibility they had landed on the shores of one of the larger ones but—after so many weeks of passing through mile after mile of wilderness places —the chance of that would be an out-and-out miracle. That being the case, they decided they might as well go to bed and tackle the problem, again, in the morning. That is, everyone except Gerald, who volunteered to sleep on the long upholstered bench at the back of the table, there in the galley, in case Stuart woke up and didn't know where he was or what had happened.

By that time, it was nearly midnight.

As exhausted as Stella was, she remembered thinking—just before she drifted off to sleep—that she had never faced any disaster with so much calm and assurance as she felt just then. Maybe it was because she never had so many people to face one with before. Then, again, it could be that having such a strong, wonderful husband (who always made the best of things) helped her feel like she could survive anything, too. Whatever it was, she knew—someplace deep in her heart—that everything would work out right. Somehow. Simply because God promised it would. It was a feeling she had never experienced, and the only reason she was able to fall into such a deep, restful sleep under such terrible circumstances. Which was a good thing.

Because it only lasted about an hour.

5

First, there was a scream (but not Millie's). Then a terrible lot of banging and commotion that seemed to be coming right down the companionway toward their door. The colonel jumped up and took off toward it in his navy pajamas (with gray piping), but Stella grabbed her white terry robe (with the Chinese collar) to put on over her rose-colored silks before following after.

She got there just in time to see Gerald tumble into the room with such a horrified expression, her first thought was that Captain Stuart had passed on and already begun to haunt them for wrecking his boat. A thought she stoutly rejected, considering her new-found faith that God could—and would—

save her from anything so frightening. If she would only ask. Except she didn't get a moment to. Not ten seconds later, a staggering form emerged out of the dark passageway and grabbed Gerald from behind, eliciting such agonizing shrieks and moans that Stella screamed (she couldn't help it), and darted behind the huge protective bulk of her husband as he grappled to separate the two.

"Here, now—what's this—what's this?" He finally managed to get in between them. "Stuart—Stuart! Everything is fine—I assure you, sir! Come over to the couch and I'll explain." Words that had a settling effect on the haggard form. Almost like a balloon slowly losing its air.

The colonel helped him over to the settee and it was then Stella noticed his right arm was dangling lifeless at his side and he was dragging a leg along like it was weighed down by some invisible ball and chain. She felt a catch in her throat that Gerald hadn't been far wrong when he guessed the man had been stricken by some sort of stroke.

"What a—ghastly experience!" Gerald whispered aside to her, and rubbed a hand over his throat at the same time. "He tried to choke me! I heard him shuffling around and—before I could even get out of my sleeping bag—he tried to choke me!"

There was another garbled moan directed at the colonel this time and it was clear he was trying to speak but couldn't manage a comprehensible word. The right side of his face seemed to have drooped and become immobile, adding a rather grotesque expression to his already rugged features. Especially with those bushy black eyebrows that nearly made a solid line across his forehead. Her husband drew in a breath and smacked his knees (she knew that decisive gesture well) before he said, "Well, sir, it seems you've had an episode of sorts."

Stuart gave out with another moan, mournful this time, and a look of abject misery crossed over his face.

"Always the possibility that symptoms are temporary however," the colonel went on. "You've been unconscious for hours. We weren't even sure you'd come back to us. But you did. A man of your strength and spirit, why, I believe—with the proper rest and care—you most certainly will recover!"

It was a statement that should have had a more calming effect on the man (it certainly did on Stella and she agreed whole-heartedly). But instead, he began to get agitated, again, banged his good arm against his leg, and tried once more to speak. At which point Millie burst in (wearing only a nightgown), with Mason not far behind, clad in sweats and a sleeveless undershirt.

"Stuart—oh, you're alive—thank God!" she cried. "We're in terrible trouble!"

A statement that caused the poor Captain to lapse into more audible frustrations.

"Mildred, for crying out loud!" said Mason. "You want to give the man a heart attack on top of it? Listen here, Stu—"

It was at that time Cole strode through the door, shirtless and barefoot, with only a pair of hastily donned jeans on. Lou Edna was close behind, also barefoot, in a long purple t-shirt that only covered the necessities, and her hair hanging loose over her shoulders. The rest of them naturally parted to let him through (he was the only one with any rank or knowledge of the sea left among them)— their new leader by unspoken consensus, even though he was young.

He leaned over to put firm hands on each of Stuart's shoulders and their eyes locked. "I had to put her on the rocks, Cap. It was too late to go around. But she can't sink. We got a hundred and thirty feet of water on one side, and eighty on the other. Little less than fifty to the shore. We're good."

A visible wave of relief came over him.

"Too closed-in for the radio, though," he went on. "Tomorrow, I'll run the skiff out into the open and try and flag down some help.

We're good." He continued to hold on for a minute as if the man might topple over if he let go, then repeated, "We're good," before he stood up straight, again.

All at once, the old captain seemed unbearably weary and it looked as if he might fall asleep, again, any minute.

"Might as well stay in my cabin," said Mason. "It's closer to everybody, and you won't have to go down any stairs. I'll bunk in with Millie. Been spending most of my time there, anyway."

So, the men helped him up and settled him there, while the women murmured their second good-nights of the long day and drifted back to their beds.

6

The following morning brought rain and wind, along with a constant current of ripples in from the choppy strait outside the inlet. The barometer was falling, signifying another weather front coming in. While it made little effect on their solidly grounded vessel, there would be no venturing out into storm- tossed seas in the little skiff to try and seek help from other passing boats. Few people would be fishing out there today, wherever they were.

But even though the day was gray and raining torrents, it was plain to see they had landed in the most beautiful, picture-postcard of a place. And although it was only August, the little meadow that stretched away into the mountains was already tinged with the red and gold hues of fall. That particular morning, there was a mother deer with two babies grazing not far away—a sight that cheered the family up considerably in spite of their dire circumstances. This was Alaska!

At any rate, it seemed to stir everyone out of the shock of the night before and it suddenly seemed clear what they should each be doing. The men were going to get seriously busy on the repairs that had only been temporarily patched and the women, having spied a huge stand of bushes fairly sagging with huckleberries close by, were going to take the little skiff into shore for a land expedition. They thought.

Not long after they announced those plans Mason established a new rule that none of them were to leave the ship without at least one of the men along. Something they all quite naturally accepted since he was an expert on survival. Not only had he lived on his own for weeks, back in the jungles of Viet Nam, but had managed to save others along with himself while he was doing it.

So it was, that Lou Edna bundled the Senator into her backpack-carrier, appropriately dressed in a tiny yellow rain-hat and slicker that made Stella think of the famous Paddington Bear, of children's literature. Was there anything more adorable? The rest of them were bundled into rain-gear as well, armed with a sufficient amount of gallon-sized plastic bags stuffed into their pockets to bring home a treasure-load of berries.

Cole came along to handle the skiff and provide the necessary male supervision their new rule required, although he made it clear—right up front—he had no desire to pick any berries. Millie made a bet with him then and there, he would be venturing into those bushes all on his own as soon as he got a taste of her "Huckleberry Betty." The windfall wouldn't be around much longer but if they took advantage of it, there would be enough berries to provide jam and desserts throughout the whole winter. Wait and see.

No one knew how to store up food, like Millie.

It took longer to get everyone over the side and situated in the skiff than to cross the fifty feet of deep water to the shore. It wasn't until then that Stella realized she hadn't set foot on land since that last Canadian town where they had found the dollar store. Almost three weeks, ago. The first thing that struck her was the delicious smell of the air. It was a combination of pine trees, rich earth, and the sea.

Cole set out for the top of a nearby hill to have a look at the waterfall but promised to not be more than a shout away in case they needed him. Lou Edna took the baby carrier off her shoulders and set it down in such a way that provided a perfect perch for the Senator to enjoy a morning snack of graham crackers and watch the festivities. It was at that point Millie briefly unfastened her raincoat to get at all her plastic bags, when Stella noticed she had a huge leather holster with a pearl- handled gun sticking out, strapped to her waist, underneath.

"It's a specially-made, three-fifty-seven magnum," she replied to Stella's sudden gasp. "My first husband bought it for me back in our prepper days."

"Good grief, Millie—can you actually shoot it?"

"Of course I can shoot it. Took lessons, and everything. I'm a pretty good shot, too, even if I say so, myself. Wouldn't want to run into any bears without it."

The thought suddenly occurred to Stella that she better inform Cole about this before he got too far away. She would tell him to be sure and make plenty of noise coming and going, so he wouldn't get mistaken for a bear. Something that would also give any nearby bears a warning to keep their distance, as well. She did not want her friend take a pot-shot at one (that didn't hit home) and only make it mad. Stella had read enough bear stories to know such things happened more often than not when all parties had their attentions distracted by berries.

But it wasn't so easy to catch up with Cole and she finally had to call out to him. He turned around and waited for her. It wasn't until they were close enough that she noticed how upset he looked. Maybe he and Lou Edna had argued, again.

"Sorry to break in on your quiet time," she spoke first. "But I thought I should warn you to make plenty of noise on your way back because Millie's packing a gun."

He murmured something Stella didn't quite catch under his breath and shook his head. "If there's one thing I got to say about this group, it's nobody's boring." He sat down on a large, nearby rock and looked out at the view... a gray desolate expanse of rock-strewn inlet (so many of them were visible now that it was low tide), and the *Dreadnaught* perched on the tallest cluster, like some giant bird with a broken wing. "Did anyone tell her you can't drop a bear with some lady's pea-shooter?"

"Oh, it isn't a pea-shooter. It's a... what was it, now... oh, yes. A three-fifty-seven magnet."

He laughed, and shook his head, again.

"Anyway, that's what I thought she said." Stella sat down next to him. "Of course, I've read a lot of Louis L'Amore westerns and know most handguns aren't accurate at long distances. Either way, it's an accident waiting to happen, so maybe you should holler out before you come down. So you don't startle her."

"Thanks. I'll do that."

He was quiet for so long that she got to her feet, again. "Mrs. H?"

"Yes?"

"How did a person like you end up getting mixed up in all this?"

"Well, I guess you could say I had the fine

good fortune to get a second chance at life. So, even with these, umm...unusual circumstances, I'm still having a marvelous time."

"You think you can forgive me for being so rough with Cap?"

"Well, of course I forgive you. I admit I was shocked to see you push him like that. But..."

"I had to get him off the wheel. He was stuck to it like rigor mortis set in and I knew we were gonna hit."

"Oh, I understand all that, now. The colonel says we would have sunk if you hadn't run us up onto the rocks so hard. On account of it being so deep around here."

"We'd have lost everything if we did. Gerald and Buddy... they never would have made it up from below fast enough. Even if they had, that water's way too cold for either of them."

Stella suddenly realized how sensitive he was. Funny how tender hearts were often housed in the toughest of bodies. And she was touched that he had even taken her suggestion and come up with a name of his own to call the Senator, the way all the rest of them had. He seemed to have taken on the responsibility of actually being a father to the little boy. As far as Lou Edna would allow anyway. "It was exactly the right thing to do, Cole. I find it amazing you could even think that fast."

"Sorry I had to be so hard on Cap, though. Didn't mean to cause him any brain damage." He shook his head and looked out at the view, again. "I love that old man!"

"You did not cause brain damage," she replied firmly. "His brain was starting to misfire before we even got here. Millie noticed it over a week, ago. She mentioned it to me."

"Well, getting shoved on his ear didn't help it any. Thing is, I lost my folks early. Been hanging around waterfronts— working my tail off—since I was fourteen. He's the only one ever gave me any kind of break. The only one. I just..." He took a deep breath and leaned his forearms across his knees. "I just wish I could have done better for him."

Stella sat down next to him and rubbed a comforting hand across his broad shoulder. "I think he knows that. You're the one he responds most to. The one who doesn't patronize, and tells him the absolute truth. If you ask me, I'd say he feels the same way about you."

"Well, you can bet I'm going to take care of him for the rest of his life. Because what he did for me? I don't take that light. Lou and I talked about it and we both feel the same—"

There was a loud, resounding blast, a startled yelp from Lou Edna, and the baby started to cry.

"Holy—crud!" He leaped to his feet. "She better either missed it—or killed it!"

Stella didn't even try to keep up with him as he took off down the hill. But if it had been anything serious there would have been a lot more hollering and screaming by now.

Instead, Mason's voice boomed over the water from the after-deck where he was working, "Mildred—what did I tell you about that thing!"

"I thought I saw something in that tall grass up there, Mase! False alarm."

Stella breathed a sigh of relief as she picked her way down the incline at her own careful pace. It was a lot easier going up than down. All at once, she saw someone stick their head up out of the grassy meadow a short distance away and their eyes met with the same identical expression. Who on earth? Before she realized it was the head and shoulders of a bear. Her first thought was that it had such intelligent eyes. Almost like a person's. What a shame it would be to kill such a creature!

"Go! Go that way!" she whispered, pointing in the opposite direction before continuing on her own way down the hill. Oddly enough, the bear—almost as if it understood—moved off toward the trees just as quickly. It wasn't until later that she realized she hadn't felt even a flutter of fear.

Another miracle!

7

The weather front hung in place, pouring a deluge of rain down on top of the castaways for an entire week. During that time they discovered more accurately how long it would take to get the boat operational again, and then off the rocks. If no help came it could take weeks. And though they had plenty of resources aboard for repairs—knowing the lodge would most likely be in terrible shape from having been vacant for so many years—they didn't know exactly what kind of place that was, or if it even still existed. For all they knew it could be nothing more than a tumble-down shack sitting in the middle of some swamp.

So, they had some decisions to make.

The majority of which really belonged to Stuart. They had dragged the man from one end of the ship to the other, lowering him over the side in a "bo'sun's chair" to see the damage, or even bundled into his rain gear to get a look at the work area they had set up on shore.

A make-shift bridge had been constructed early on by felling two trees and then hammering short pieces of wood across the top for a boardwalk. Something that saved a considerable amount of time and effort in hauling things back and forth between the boat and the shore.

On the occasions Stuart needed to come across, Cole simply hoisted him onto his back in a "Fireman's Carry" and hustled him over the bridge to his supervisor chair. It was one of the deck chairs tucked under a tarp-covered area where Mason had set up the portable sawmill he brought along for making lumber. They had been making lumber ever since they got there. It soon became evident that the Captain's mind was as sharp as ever. He had only lost the ability to speak or move around easily. A situation that still occasionally threw him into a rage of frustration. One that almost always simmered down somewhat with a reassuring clap on the shoulder from the colonel, and the remark, "It's only temporary, sir—only temporary!"

However, it was Stella, and her many years of having to deal with mentally deranged people, who had come up with the ingenious system of communication that worked best for him. She did it by keeping several washable markers at the table. The ones Millie used for the little white-board tacked up in the pantry to keep track of stores. A different color for each member of the family.

The large wooden dining table was lacquered so smooth that it made the perfect surface for him to write or draw on, then erase with a damp cloth. And even though it often turned into a game of Charades, trying to figure out what he meant (his right hand was not usable, so he had to struggle with his left), it was at least immediately apparent by which color he picked up, who that particular message was for. That and a few gestures, such as a nod or shake of the head for yes, or no. Thus, he was reinstated as the top-ranking voting member of the party.

So it was, that he sat at the head of the table (it was their first Sunday afternoon since the disaster), armed with his markers and a cup of tea poured into one of the Senator's "sippy cups" (most liquid he drank tended to leak out the slack side of his mouth, otherwise) and—on this occasion—a notebook and pencil. Signifying he was going to attempt to communicate something important.

The meeting was called to order.

"What a blessing we've brought our own little world into the wilderness with us," observed the colonel, as he finished off the last bit of Millie's Huckleberry Betty. "To be in a situation like this and still have the sort of comforts we enjoy aboard the *Dreadnaught*. Light, warmth, superb food, and the coziest of homes...mmm! Must be a sermon in that, somewhere."

"Speaking of such," said Mason, helping himself to another cup of coffee, "you being the most educated on that subject, I was thinking how it would do us all good, under the circumstances, to share some of what you been talking to Shortcake about. I'm ashamed every time I have to agree she's right, lately."

"It's just I have a lot of questions, Pop. I've been doing things wrong my whole life. And Mr. Colonel says—"

The baby, who was standing on the upholstered bench between her and Cole, suddenly stopped playing with the Jello boxes Millie had given him, and leaned against her to jabber into her ear.

"The colonel says," she repeated as she automatically stacked the boxes into a tower for him, again, "the only way you can change your wrong thinking is by learning what's right. Then practicing that until God miraculously changes your mind."

"I believe that's a Lou Edna paraphrase for Romans 12:2," the colonel interjected. "Where it states we can actually be transformed by the renewing of our minds. Once again, it's a decision we all individually have to make."

"All I know is it took a miracle to change me." The toddler knocked his boxes down again, and she reached under the table to pick two off the floor.

"Like I always said," replied Mason. "Didn't think you'd ever change, since I thought it couldn't be done. Anyway, a little Bible reading on Sundays wouldn't hurt any of us. Right, Stuart?"

The Captain shrugged, but only one shoulder went up.

"He doesn't mind," interpreted Gerald.

"Then it would be an honor," the colonel agreed.

"All right, then." Mason took a folded piece of paper out of the pocket of his red and black flannel shirt. "Now for the items up for a vote."

Millie stopped wiping off the stove and came to sit down next to him. Stella linked her arm through the colonel's and sighed with contentment as she looked at the whole family seated around the table.

"First up, we have to decide whether we should just stay right here for the winter. Point being we don't know when, or if, we're going to get help. If so, there's things we can do before the cold weather comes to make it more comfortable around here. Such as blocking the back end of the boat up, so we can get rid of this cock-eyed slant we been walking around on. Thing is, it would take some time away from repairs to do it."

"If we do get help," said Gerald, "I volunteer to go with Stuart, so he can get some medical. Or, at least some therapy on..." His hand involuntarily felt for his throat. "How to deal with all this."

The Captain tossed the green marker at him with his left hand and bounced it off his head.

"Oh, I say!" Gerald replaced it in the pile.

"We'll cross that bridge when we come to it," said Mason. "Any opinions up for discussion?"

"Well," Millie spoke first. "Considering our original plan— before E.J. let us off— was to disappear somewhere in Alaska, it's not like we didn't come prepared to do something like this. The only hard thing is being totally cut off from the rest of the world. Which is something we can't do anything about right now, anyway. So... I vote, yes."

"Me, too," agreed Stella. "We came to experience Alaska, and this is about Alaska as it can get."

"It would definitely give me enough time to finish my novel," the colonel put it. "Might be rather freeing, not writing to a deadline for once. I couldn't accept a contract on speculation, now, even if I wanted to. No Internet, no telephone, no post office. I vote, yes, as well."

"So, it's down to the DeForio family, then," said Mason.

"This is the best I ever had it," Cole admitted.

"I don't care what we do," Lou Edna added. "If I didn't have this family, I'd have killed myself by now."

"For heaven sake, Lou," Millie admonished. "Don't give me such a start this early in the discussion."

"Well, it's true."

"Stuart?" Mason looked over in time to see another one-shouldered shrug.

"He doesn't mind," said Gerald.

"Passed. Point number two. It occurred to me we should establish a signal fire. Could be we got ourselves farther off than we thought and ended up buried into some national wilderness area no one ever goes to much."

Stuart gave out with a bellow and reached for Mason's red marker. But instead of writing anything, he merely jabbed at the air over the top of the carpenter's head with it.

"Oh, right." Mason raised up in his seat enough to get the last chart they had been navigating by, that was rolled up and stashed behind the back of the bench. "Stu thinks we're somewhere around..." He slid the rubber band off and unrolled it for everyone to see. "Here."

He pointed to a cluster of little islands off the southwest tip of the Alexander Archipelago, that lay between the Pacific Ocean, the West Dixon Entrance, and the South Prince of Wales Wilderness. Ketchikan was at least sixty miles to the northeast, and the nearest other town was... they all stared silently at the vast amount of space... the closest seemed to be a logging camp, situated on the largest island. But that was even farther away than Ketchikan.

"That being the case," Mason went on, "a

continuously burning fire might be the only thing that would catch anyone's attention this far out. At least by some passing plane that could report it to the Forest Service, maybe. So..." He looked up at the group, again. "We got to set fire watches throughout the day to man it. Two at a time is best, in case of..." He rubbed a hand over his three-day growth of salt-and-pepper whiskers. "Something happens."

"Lou and I will do the early watch," said Cole. That way I can take the skiff out the inlet before the tide changes and look for any boats out there."

"I hate early mornings," complained Lou.

"You just haven't seen enough of them," Cole replied.

"OK. Cole and Lou on the first one, then." Mason wrote it down on the back of his list. "Who's next?"

After they had each chosen their times for the fire watch, the third order of the day was the announcement of their need to conserve diesel.

"But, why?" Millie asked. "We're not even going anywhere."

"Because the generator that makes your electricity runs off diesel," he answered. "And—in case you haven't noticed— there wasn't a lick of sun, this week to use Stuart's solar- powered system. Not to mention we're in the middle of a rainforest, here. So, it could be like this most of the time from now on."

"Oh."

"I imagine we're running close to empty, anyway," the colonel pointed out, "since we haven't added any since we left California. Thought it better to have a bit of a money cushion for an emergency fund when we got here, as I recall."

"We've definitely got ourselves an emergency," said Gerald. "But who'd have thought it would end up being gas?" It was at that point the Captain began growling and fussing, until he was fairly spitting with frustration, in an effort to find something in his notebook. "Mah—Bo!" he finally sputtered out. "Mah—Bo!"

"Of course, it's your boat, my good man," the colonel replied, though he was too far across the table to clap him on the shoulder. "It will always be your boat, sir!"

"Mah—Bo—" He repeated louder and slower, reaching at the same time for his black marker.

Cole jumped to his feet (black being his color) and moved behind him to look over his shoulder. One, two, three vertical lines, and... an upside down M. Or, maybe it was a W. Then came an A, and eventually a T.

"Wah...wat..." Cole ran a hand through his wavy hair and concentrated harder. "Maybe he wants us to conserve water." At which point the older man pulled his Captain's hat off and smacked his First Mate over the head with it.

"Cripes, Cap—give me another hint, then!"

"We could be getting low on water." Stella was thinking how much she enjoyed her evening shower. "Seems we haven't topped off since we were half-way through Canada."

"Not a problem," said Mason, "since we have the waterfall so close by."

"Wah—Fah!" the Captain thundered, with a resounding crash of his fist against the table that shook all their dishes.

"Waterfall!" Cole called it out as if it had been just before the buzzer in the game of Charades. "OK, waterfall. Geeze. What about it?"

Stuart flipped through his notebook then until he came to a very sketchy sketch that he shoved out into the center of the table for all of them to see.

"Reminds me of one of A.J.'s first wife's preliminary modern art sketches," Gerald mused, as they all stared at it. "The ones Lou got so much money for."

The Captain pointed at three parallel lines which looked similar to the three he had drawn on the table. He pulled Cole closer by the sleeve of his denim shirt, then thumped a spot on the paper that could have been a child's rendition of a sunshine face. The kind teacher's put on their papers for good work. "Mah —Bo," he insisted. Then smacked him on the shoulder, thumped the paper, again, and raised his voice. "Mah—Bo!"

They started building the "Mah-Bo," as it came to be called, the very next day.

After a great deal more deliberation the night before, Cole had suddenly recalled the Captain talking to him about alternative power systems and showing him a folder that was fairly bursting with articles cut out of magazines that he had been collecting for years. At the time, they had been discussing alternative fuels and the different modifications one would have to make to engines in order to even use them. However, a light went on when he remembered that incident, and he went down below to rifle through one of the shelves above Stuart's workbench to get the folder.

True to his guess, the Captain's face lit up, and it wasn't long before they found the blueprints for a homemade, electricity-producing, waterwheel. Something similar to what used to be seen on old mills. The way Stuart laughed (it was the first time since his episode) and kept repeating, "Mah-Bo!" and slapping Cole on the back half a dozen times, it was only natural that they should end up calling the contraption a Mah-Bo.

Once they knew what they were doing, everybody chipped in to help, and it was only a little over a week before the huge wheel was built, and the thing was operational. Mason had brought enough tools along to build a city. Of course, there were a few modifications that had to be made to run the wiring in and out of nearby trees, and over the fifty-foot span of water. But they now had their own power station that could produce all the electricity they would ever need. Including outside lights along the handrails of the bridge, that made it look like the entrance to a ride at Disneyland.

It was something that put even more of a cushion between them and the wild outside that surrounded them. In fact, very little had changed about their basic lifestyle since they had left *Villa Nofre*, the old Hollywood director's mansion in the beautiful Santa Ynez Mountains, back in California. The little group was actually discovering more opportunities in the unexpected situation, rather than setbacks.

Because of the increasing rain, any work area was fitted with a canopy of brown tarps. Soon, the side of the boat where damaged planks were being replaced, the after-deck, and the sawmill were crowned with them. Combined with the rope handrails that had been added to the boardwalk bridge (ever since Gerald had fallen halfway in when a foot slipped), the place was beginning to look like a movie set instead of a work area. Especially with the *Dreadnaught*, grounded on top of the rocks, like a shipwrecked pirate's vessel, rather than the family's rambling home. Shipboard duties had long since given way to building improvements, and even the bell that had called all hands on deck, rang out primarily only at mealtimes.

They had even put together a three-sided wooden shelter (with a tarp on top) that faced their huge signal fire. Where those on fire watch could sit comfortably in deck chairs and stay dry. Stella found it amazing how a fire could be kept going in the rain. But as long as the wood was dry and it was burning hot enough, they could at least keep smoke going up in all but the heaviest downpours. Which was the important thing. Because once they got into the latter part of August, there seemed to be more rainy days than sunny ones.

Cole had ventured out a few times in the skiff, but so far he had never seen a single fishing boat. Too many small islands and rock outcroppings at the end of the cape that made working anywhere close to the area hazardous. But he still continued to try. He did come back with a beautiful forty-five pound halibut, the last time, though. Which, after a meal fit for royalty, Millie had packed the rest into the freezer, to be doled out through the coming weeks. It was after this feast that Stella and the colonel found themselves seated in the "fire hut" for the final watch of the day, that would last until sunset. An event that took place around eight-thirty, these days.

"Well, dearest," the colonel began as he poured them each a mug of hot chocolate from a tall metal thermos, "this isn't exactly how we expected to end our honeymoon. But it's an experience I'm sure we'll never forget."

"Even with the scary parts it's been the best experience I've ever had, Oliver. I think I could live through being stranded on the moon as long as you were there."

"I feel the same way, too, Stel. Being married to you is a delight I never expected to experience, at my age."

"Me, either." She blew gently on her chocolate and then tentatively took a sip. Delicious! "And wasn't it providential that Stuart got the others married before all this happened? He never would have been able to do that after his episode."

"Quite impossible. But you know I think that's half the reason everything's been going so smoothly for us, since. One always seems to feel more settled when they know things are done right."

"I agree. You know something?"

"What."

Stella breathed in the wonderful scent of campfire mingled with fresh air and pines, as she looked past the fire and out into the lovely meadow leading into the mountains, turning all gold in the setting sun. "I'm starting to like it so much here, I wouldn't really care if we never went on to the lodge. If you want to know the absolute truth about it... I don't feel the least bit lost, at all. Especially since Captain Stuart has something of an idea where we are, now."

"I've had the very same thoughts, myself." He set his cup down on the little table between them, and got up to put more wood on the fire. "I really think I've done my best work, here."

"I'm sure you have." She watched him pull a pair of work gloves out of his back pocket and put them on before hauling some of the brush and tree-trimmings they had cleared from the work areas, over to the waning flames. Funny how good physical work tended to make a person stronger rather than wearing them out. Especially if they enjoyed it. Not only was the colonel trimming down after all these weeks of adventuring, he was actually looking younger. Other than his wavy silver hair, but that just made him look distinguished. At least, that's what Stella was thinking, just then.

"You know, I wouldn't be all that disappointed if we never went back to civilization," he picked up the conversation as soon as he sat down, again. "Other than short business trips once or twice a year."

"That would be a lovely way to live, if you ask me." She suddenly lowered her voice to a whisper and pointed. "Oliver —look!"

In the far corner of the meadow a black bear was moving off into the trees. It was a wonderful moment, the two of them sharing the glimpse of a wild thing, going about its business as if they weren't there, at all.

"Do you think he sees us?" Stella asked.

"Oh, undoubtedly. But he's probably accepted that this is our territory now, so he'll keep his distance and stick to his. Seems they accept you if you give them half a chance and try to respect their space, as well."

"Mildred—put that gun down!" Mason's voice suddenly drifted across the water from the foredeck, where the two of them had also been watching the sunset.

"But I thought I saw something out there, Mase. I really did, this time!"

"We're just guests in this wilderness, so live and let live," he replied. "That's the new rule."

Author's Note

They say what one practices in their youth can never be surpassed by those who come to the same skill later in life. Such was evident in Daniel Boone (quoted at the beginning of this story), who began wandering through wilderness places on the edge of the Pennsylvania frontier, in his childhood. He received his first rifle by the age of twelve, and became (as other boys of his day) an essential contributor to the family food larder. After being persecuted in England for their dissenting beliefs, his parents (who were Quakers) emigrated to America in 1713, to join William Penn's colony. Daniel was the sixth of their eleven children.

Perhaps growing up in a large family, in a group known for their propensity to sacrifice themselves for others, is what laid the foundation for Daniel to become not only a provider and protector of his own, but other people, as well. However, having also been born during one of the most tumultuous times of American history—including the Indian wars and the Revolution—he was not destined for a life of peace.

Which is one of the things that makes him so unique. Because in spite of the many dangers, hardships and battles he faced throughout his life, he still managed—remarkably—to remain a man of strong morals, always willing to share with others, and a leader when it came to civic duties. He was elected three times to the Virginia General Assembly.

He is one of the first folk heroes of the United States, who became a legend in his own time. That unique position which comes from an admiring public who accepts the "tall tales" of a person's adventures right along with the true ones. Known best for forging and marking his famous Wilderness

Road, through the Cumberland Gap in the Appalachian Mountains (that over 200,000 pioneers later used to find their way west), he is fondly remembered as the most colorful and extraordinary frontiersman the country has ever known. Respected for generations by friend and enemy alike, it is still commonly believed that if one knew even half what Daniel Boone did in his day, they could eventually find their way out of any wilderness they happened to fall into.

And I'm inclined to agree.

You can read more about this wonderful man— for free at many places online.

About Lilly Maytree

Lilly Maytree is the author of *Gold Trap, The Pandora Box,* and *The Stella Madison Capers*. Books that sent her careening along on her "Mystery Tours" with her captain husband aboard the *Glory B.* She loves sharing these adventures with readers. It has even been said that she time-travels (but that's probably just a rumor). To find out about her current adventures, simply visit:

www.LillyMaytree.com

Home Before Dark
(Caper #1)

Here is the first of the Stella Madison Capers, the story of how everything started, and how she escaped from a catastrophe that seemed to come out of nowhere. Which is the nature of catastrophes but it's so hard to be logical when you're in the middle of one. It's also the story of how she met the colonel (if you're interested in that sort of thing).

A Thief in the House
(Caper #2)

Stella Madison is back, this time with a bevy of friends. But just how far should a person go when it comes to sticking by their friends? There's a thief in the rambling old mansion she moved into. And while it was someone who was quick to lend help when Stella needed it most, how can she possibly return the favor without jeopardizing herself along with them? No person is obligated to go that far... right?

Voyage of the Dreadnaught
collection of four Stella Madison Capers

Here is a collection of the four Stella Madison Capers covering the entire voyage of the *Dreadnaught*, through the Inside Passage to Alaska. Includes: *Sea Trials, The Pushover Plot, Lost in the Wilderness*, and *The Last Resort*. Also includes a brief account of Lilly Maytree's true-life voyage along the same route, in the sailboat *Glory B*.

For Writers...

Unspoken Rules

Popular books (those stories everyone likes no matter what the subject) all have certain things in common. And what they have most in common is what they DON'T do. Within the following pages, dear writer, you will find the three most important "don'ts" of popular fiction that I learned when I was studying the masters. Why? Because I love research and I never mind sharing my notes.

Writing Rules!
(a mysterious student handbook)

A mysterious little desktop handbook that can help anyone (well, almost anyone) with writing rules. Especially if you are a student and have to write things all the time.

For Parents...

Behave Yourself!
Teaching your children to discipline themselves.

Are you tired of bickering during daily routines encroaching on way too much of your family time? Here is a book that offers a two-week program that teaches your children to discipline themselves. Hard to believe? Here are the step-by-step secrets of how it's done, and why it works.

The Nature of Children
(And how to deal with it.)

A manual based on a compilation of parenting articles Lilly wrote over several years as a columnist for *Childcare Magazine*. It is a result of many requests from parents for more information about that content and the foundation of the methods she used both in raising her own children, and in her classrooms.

After years of experience, she has a lot to say about what motivates children and has implemented many of her unique ideas into books and programs that others can use.

For autographed copies, visit:

www.LillyMaytree.com

Excerpt from

The Last Resort

Stella Madison Caper #5

Lilly Maytree

To all those who think they have nothing significant or worthwhile to offer—or that it's too late even if they did…may you know that it isn't.

"To each there comes in their lifetime a special moment when they are figuratively tapped on the shoulder and offered the chance to do a very special thing, unique to them and fitted to their talents. What a tragedy if that moment finds them unprepared or unqualified for that which could have been their finest hour."

Winston Churchill

Stella Madison had been doing her morning exercise routine for so long she could do it without thinking. Which was exactly what she was up to that morning when the colonel interrupted her standing pushups to inform her that he had a "plot knot" to work out.

"Stel," he began before he even crossed the deck to stand beside her at the stern rail, "I've got the boys in something of a predicament. Are you up for a bit of brainstorming?"

"Of course, dear," she replied without even breaking her rhythm. "Two heads are better than one, I always say. Twelve, fourteen, fifteen! Set up the scene for me and I'll see if I can see something from a different angle."

"Excellent." He clapped his hands together and began to pace. "They've been in the cave for three days, now. So far, there's been no sign of—"

"Heavens..." she turned toward the mountain to starboard, kept a firm hold on the rail, and began her leg raises. "Are they lost?"

"Not at all, they're exploring. You see, it's imperative they find another way out before—"

"But wouldn't their parents worry? Thirteen, fifteen, sixteen... I mean, three whole days..."

"Oh, they aren't that young." He reached the port rail and turned to pace back in her direction, again. "Quite capable, really. Which is one of the main thrusts of the whole book." He jabbed at the air for example. "But you're right. Maybe I should emphasize it more at this point to keep that thought in the forefront."

"Especially for these difficult times we live in." She turned to face the mountain on their port side and continue with her other leg. "Seems like people are afraid of everything, nowadays."

"Right, again."

"You know, Oliver...(twenty-one, twenty-three, twenty- four...), as I've been reading along each day, I didn't get the feeling they were that old. Thirteen, or fourteen, is what I thought. That's how I've been picturing them, anyway. Twenty- five, twenty-eight, twenty-nine, thirty!" She flopped over from the waist, arched her back, and then slowly raised up, again, with a whisper of, "two, three!"

"Yes, they're in their early teens. I believe I even mentioned as much back at the beginning somewhere."

"I think young people are a lot more immature than we used to be at their age, don't you?"

"Definitely. That's part of the problem, of course. Being capable of so much more than they are actually allowed to do."

Stella flopped back down and began to come up slowly, again. "I couldn't agree more. Six, seven, eight!"

The colonel suddenly stopped and turned before he got to the opposite rail, this time. "Do you realize how many numbers you're skipping?"

"What?"

"Your counting, dearest. It's all over the place."

"Oh, that. Well, it doesn't matter so much. As long as I do six of each."

"Is there some reason why you don't just count to six and start over, again?"

"Not really. Except it wouldn't be half as encouraging as the higher numbers."

She knew by the way his silver eyebrows squeezed toward each other and his lower lip jutted out, that he didn't get the connection. But instead of arguing, or even trying to convince her to see things his way, he said, "Where were we?"

"In the cave." She began to run in place. Light, quick, bouncy steps. How wonderful it was to be married to a man who wasn't forever insisting she explain everything. "For three whole days!"

At which point there was a tremendous crash. The deck tipped at a crazy angle for a few seconds, followed by a resounding thud, and the two of them suddenly found themselves sliding on their backsides toward the lower rail. Without a thing they could do about it.

Stella screamed (she couldn't help it) at the same time she felt the colonel reach out and grab hold enough to keep her from tumbling over the side. Not that she hadn't always considered herself a fairly good swimmer. But this was Alaska! Where it was rumored one couldn't last much more than fifteen minutes in such cold water without slipping into something called hypothermia.

"Mason—Jeffries!" Millie bawled from the galley. "You just dropped my applesauce bread flatter than a pancake!" Stella saw her friend's auburn head come poking through a nearby porthole just as the colonel was helping her to her feet. "You're supposed to warn us before you do that kind of stuff!"

"I didn't do anything," the carpenter called back from across the little bridge that connected the *Dreadnaught* to the shore. "Been over here making lumber all morning." Then he came closer to look at the lopsided angle their ship was now tilted at. "What the... devil!"

A few minutes later, the door to the port companionway flung open and Millie's cousin, Gerald, staggered out with his orange life-jacket only hanging around his neck, and not tied. "Are we sinking?" He flung a look over the rail. "I say—there's a hole bigger than a garage door down below!"

End of Excerpt

To read the rest of this Stella Madison Caper, visit us online at:

LightsmithPublishers.com

*Also available from Ingram
wherever books are sold.*

If you enjoyed reading this
"Little Traveling Book"
please share it with someone!

If you have children (or know any),
you may even enjoy browsing the
"mysteriously different books" over at:

SummersIslandPress.com